To all the dedicated educators who help military children
realize their full potential.

We salute you!

The mission of the Jackson in Action 83 Foundation is to provide support to
military families, focusing on the educational, emotional, and physical health
of the children. To learn more about the foundation, visit
www.jacksoninaction83.org. Proceeds from the sales of this book directly
benefit military families who serve on the front lines, both abroad and at home.

To all the brave men and women who selflessly serve and protect our nation
and to their families for their strength and sacrifices.

Thank you,
Lindsey & Vincent Jackson

www.mascotbooks.com

Danny Dogtags: A Cool School Story

For more information, please contact:
Mascot Books
620 Herndon Parkway #320
Herndon, VA 20170
info@mascotbooks.com

Library of Congress Control Number: 2019915187

CPSIA Code: PRT1219A
ISBN-13: 978-1-68401-935-9

Printed in the United States

Danny Dogtags
A Cool School Story

Written by Lindsey and Vincent Jackson

Illustrated by Omar Hechtenkopf

Danny's dad had just been assigned orders to a new town so Danny and his family had to move.

It was a very pretty town, with lots of trees and lakes and parks, but something felt strange to Danny.

"Are you excited for your first day at school?" Danny's mom asked.

"I don't know," said Danny as he grabbed the lunch his mom had packed for him. "I'm kind of nervous. I don't know anyone at this school."

Danny, his mom, and his dad walked to the bus stop down the street from their house. Danny dragged his feet even though he knew it could only delay them for so long.

"There's nothing to be nervous about," Danny's dad said. "Just be yourself, and you'll be fine. I'm sure you'll make some new friends quickly. You did great at your last school, remember?"

"Yeah, but that was a while ago," said Danny. "What if I can't remember how to do it again?"

Just then, the bus pulled up. Danny took a deep breath, waved bye to his parents, and got on.

Luckily, there was an empty seat near the back of the bus. Danny slid into it quickly. As the bus drove away, he reached for the dog tags hanging around his neck and rubbed them in his hands. He had worn these dog tags ever since his dad went on his first deployment. His dad had told Danny to rub them anytime he missed him or faced something new.

When the bus got to school, all the kids hurried off and headed to class. Danny didn't know where to go, so he rubbed his dog tags again and looked for someone to ask.

"Excuse me," said Danny to a boy who was nearby. "Do you know where I can find classroom 104?"

"That's where I'm going!" said the boy. "Follow me. I'm Lewis."

"Thanks," said Danny. "I'm new here. My name's Danny."

As they walked down the hall, Danny noticed something familiar hanging around Lewis's neck. "Are those dog tags?"

"Sure are," said Lewis. "My mom's in the Air Force."

Danny held up his dog tags and smiled. "My dad's in the Army!"

"Quiet down, class. We have a new student to welcome. Everyone please say hello to Danny Dogtags," said Danny's new teacher. The class gave Danny a warm welcome.

"Why don't you have a seat at the empty desk next to Lewis?" said Danny's teacher.

"Yes sir," said Danny as he headed to his seat. He smiled at Lewis's familiar face.

"Our project today is on the history of different European flags," their teacher explained. "Everyone, please get into pairs, and I'll come around and assign the flag you'll be studying."

Danny turned to Lewis, hoping he didn't have a partner already. "Can we work together?" he asked.

"Sure!" said Lewis. "I'll scoot my desk closer to yours."

"Hi, Lewis and Danny," said their teacher as he stopped at their desks. "You guys will be working on the German flag. Here are some books to help you do research. We'll present at the end of class. Let me know if you have any questions, and good luck!"

"Germany!" Danny exclaimed excitedly. "I know all about Germany, Lewis. We got this!"

"How do you know so much about Germany?" Lewis asked
as he pulled out his markers and a sheet of paper.
"I'll draw the flag for us."

"I lived there for a few years when I was little," said Danny. "My dad was
stationed there when I was born, so we lived on base before we moved back to
the States. He always wore these dog tags there."

"Wow, cool," said Lewis as he colored the middle stripe in the flag red. "My mom gave me hers in Colorado, where I was born. I bet you know everything about Germany!"

"Well, not everything but a thing or two!" said Danny as he opened the books their teacher had brought them. "I'll prepare our facts, and we can practice reading them together."

Danny and Lewis sat patiently as their classmates presented all sorts of colorful flags and facts from countries all over the world. Danny couldn't wait to talk about what he knew and show the class Lewis's great drawing.

"And the flag from Switzerland looks like a plus sign!" finished the girls who were presenting.

"Wonderful," said their teacher.
"Danny, Lewis, you guys are up next!"

Danny and Lewis held up the flag proudly as they began.

"As you can see," said Lewis, "the colors of the German flag are black, red, and gold."

"The current flag has been in place since 1990," said Danny, "when the coat of arms was removed after the fall of the Berlin Wall."

"Danny used to live in Germany," added Lewis, "so he's been to Berlin! Isn't that cool?"

Danny and Lewis flew through the rest of the presentation easily. When they were done, the class clapped loudly. Danny couldn't believe how comfortable he was in front of the class.

"Great job, Danny and Lewis!" their teacher said. "That was a wonderful history lesson."

After school, Danny and Lewis sat next to each other on the bus ride home.

"So where else have you lived?" asked Lewis.

"We've lived all over," said Danny, "but I especially liked living in Hawaii. The beach was our backyard! One time I almost lost my dog tags in the ocean when I was swimming. What about you? Where have you lived?"

"No way!" said Lewis. "We lived in Hawaii when my mom was stationed there, too!"

Danny and Lewis passed the rest of the bus ride talking and laughing about all their favorite things in Hawaii.

As the bus came to the stop, Danny saw his parents waiting for him. "This is my stop," he said. "See you tomorrow, Lewis!"

After Danny got off, he looked back at the bus and waved goodbye.

"Did you make a new friend?" Danny's mom asked.

"Yep!" Danny said cheerfully. "His mom is in the Air Force, and he has dog tags just like me. We did a project on the German flag together, and it went great!"

"Good work, Danny!" said his dad. "I think you'll do just fine here!"

"I think so, too," said Danny. "I can't wait to make more new friends tomorrow!"

Pro Bowl wide receiver Vincent Jackson launched the Jackson in Action 83 Foundation in 2012 as a way to support and encourage the men and women of the U.S. Armed Forces and their families. As the son of two military parents, Vincent personally understands the dedication and sacrifice required of all family members in support of a loved one's military service.